Sorry it's late, but I mean to say, when you're getting on a bit and the arthritis is setting in, Time passes pretty slowly,

from " Young Fergus".

Happy Birthday!

THE DAY OF THE GROCER

The Author (Old Twinkletoes himself) would like to thank Rowan Ayers and all at 'Late Night Line-up' for (a) housing him on their programme and (b) the use of certain jokes and notions hereinafteryet.

All the characters in this book should be fictitious, but what can you do?

William Rushton

THE DAY OF THE GROCER

 ANDRE DEUTSCH

To Sam and Matt and Tobe.
The Revolution starts here

First published 1971 by
André Deutsch Limited
105 Great Russell Street, London WC1

Printed in Great Britain by
Tonbridge Printers Ltd
Tonbridge, Kent

ISBN 0 233 96268 9

Epilogue Part 1

'Fuck me,' thought Mr Justice Trigg from his vantage point high above the Centre Court at the Old Bailey, 'She's got bloody good titties for her age.'

He groped about him. Somewhere he knew in the grubby reaches of his robes was his old black cap. A little green now, it had a corner missing where Rex had torn it from the pocket of his golf-bag. A relic it had seemed to be then – a thing of the past. Until, he remembered with a half smile that caused a murmur in the Press Gallery, even as old Rex worried at it on the hearth-rug, an excited Jacko had rung him from the Club.

'Nipper, Nipper, guess what? Just got the buzz from Quint – we're getting the rope back.'

'I don't believe it,' he had said. How could he believe it? The times he had prayed for it. But now? At this juncture? Poor, poor Alice, he had thought. There *is* no justice. 'Just before your biggie with Alice, eh?' said Jacko. She *was* guilty as hell. No doubt of that.

'We're having a bit of a piss-up tomorrow soir,' Jacko went on. 'See you there doubtless.'

'Rex! Rex!' he had called and saved the very damp cap that – dry now, but still well-chewed – he slowly placed upon his head.

'Alice Grace Henry Foulbeach, it is my solemn duty to inform you that in that you did assassinate the then Prime Minister not once but twice in manner most vile and untoward, ye shall be taken from this place and after due pause and at the Queen's pleasure, hanged by the neck until ye be extremely dead. May the Lard forgive us for we are very silly.'

Lady Foulbeach gracefully inclined the lovely neck which Public Hangman Forbes must so soon break in the pursuit of his duty.

'God bless you, Nipper,' she said in the soft voice which had coaxed forth his youthful seed so many years ago. 'Never mind.'

Mr Justice Trigg cried openly into his posy. Oh Alice, Alice, whose ample breasts had been his two best friends in happier days. Why? Why? And her gentle voice seemed to reply, 'Why not? . . . '

Chapter 1

The then Prime Minister closed the door of Number Ten behind the last visitor. He was at last alone with his triumph. He leant back against the door and sighed deeply. On the floor, where only yesterday his predecessor's hall table had stood, lay some heavily embossed envelopes, the cards of various ambassadors and prelates, firms of Mini-Cabs and Carpet Cleaners, keys and bills to be forwarded. It can all wait until tomorrow, he thought. What he needed now was somewhere to sit and think. He walked towards the stairs with the careful, measured tread of a man to whom the cruel sea is no stranger. Finally on the third floor he found the old Nursery and in it a rocking-chair. Touching what at first he took to be the light switch, he heard a bell ring floors below. He found the switch. The darkness did not budge. No bulb.

'Up him,' he said out loud. He lowered himself heavily into the rocker. The shouting and the tumult dies . . . he smiled. He had learnt that at Grammar. If only he had learnt the second line, but there had been so much else to do. Was it something about the captains and the kings having to leave? Play up, play up and play the game? And so he had. And won. And WON! With a wild whoop he hurled Bonar Law's teddy out of the open window. Only *he* had

kept the Faith. Against all the odds. And the sods.
Only he had been convinced of Victory. In a land
that prized margarine more than butter, fish fingers
higher than sole bonne femme, he had been certain
of success.

There came a knock at the door. 'Ahoy,' he
cried, and through the darkness discerned a tiny
figure.

'Who are you when you're at home?' It was a little
woman, he knew that at once.

'I am the new Prime Minister,' he boomed.

'That's very nice I'm sure, not but that I'M not the
last to know.' The little woman was eyeing him
quizzically. 'There's rissoles, but I expect *you* have
your quirks.'

Anger flickered across his deeply tanned forehead.
Many would come to be wary of that sudden flush.

'I have no quirks at all, you bloody woman! Get
out! There's a new broom at the helm NEOW –
blast - NOW!! There is going to be - ' he hesitated
and in that split second, such is the stuff of History,
his Muse exploded and some earth stood still near
Droitwich. 'There is going to be –' he said and his
mighty shoulders began to move like some gigantic
bellows, 'a Quiet Revolution!' With that he began to
turn round and round very slowly.

London slept under a Tory moon. In the old
Nursery at Number Ten, the Prime Minister slept

8

deeply on the mauve tiger-skin that lay surrounded by the rails of Clement Attlee's old train set. He dreamed of the New Tomorrow.

Dawn. And in a dainty basement flat in Kilburn, Errol 'Thud' Miller, seeded fourth at the previous Wimbledon, clambered wearily off the lean brown body of Adelaide La Perouse, where he was seeded about twenty-seventh, and sank gratefully onto his richly freckled back.

'Game set and I hope for Christ's sake they still match,' he said in his rich Australian brogue. She eyed him coldly.

'I thought you said you were very big Down Under.' Whoever said Hell hath no fury like Mrs R. P. Bradley of 14, The Glebe, Orpington, had never met the lovely Adelaide, Queensland's Own Southern Star, on the morning after. Thud thought of telling her a joke, but none came to mind. 'What's up?' he said to the same cold eye. 'I'm sorry, Adelaide, but – I mean you could make a statue ejaculate – but I went five sets with Kenny last night in Dusseldorf, four sets in the afternoon with Fred and a doubles in Paris, and it's the Swedish Championships tonight and bloody Monte on Sunday.'

'You can't tell your tennis bum from your tennis elbow,' and she was out of bed in one of those sinuous movements that had made a number of Cistercians in Surfer's Paradise look at their vows afresh.

'It's no bleeding life on the circuit, love.' He trailed her to the bathroom.

'I wonder if there's any known cure for Tennis Cock?' she enquired, stepping under the shower. He stepped in after her, screamed and stepped briskly out.

'Jeeze, you like it hot.' There was no reaction in the steam.

'Will youse marry I,' he tried.

This time a head appeared.

'How many times have I got to tell you, Thud dear, that if I'm going to stay here the Home Office says I've got to marry an Englishman within six months or back to dear old Brissie with my tail between my legs.' And here Fact *is* stranger than Fiction, for she did indeed enjoy, as did a host of her admirers, this anatomical rarity.

'Well, you've only got to slip some pom fifty quid.'

'Thud, it may come as a surprise to you but I look for a lot more in a marriage. Love, for instance. Or money.'

'Well, you always get what you want, Adelaide.'

'Not always, but this time I will.'

'Got anyone in mind then?' Thud pulled on a T-Shirt, aptly worded NEW BALLS PLEASE.

'Not yet, but my horoscope's promising.' She threw him a wet *Telegraph*. The front page was even more promising.

BRITAINS MOST ELIGIBLE BATCHELOR MOVES INTO No. 10 it said, just like that, right out loud, bloody rude, but neither of them read it. Thud was lost in the sports pages, and Adelaide was engrossed in a Peregrine Worsthorne interview with Rolf Harris.

The electric toothbrush was sending shocks of excitement through his strong white molars. It seems, he thought, to charge my brain. Today is the New Tomorrow, I hand out the jobs to the boys and my beloved Bechstein arrives from the Albany. He turned off his brush and rinsed it under the tap. He spat ruminatively into the clean, white basin. There was a speck of blood. Nicked a gum, he thought, and steadied himself against the basin as his head momentarily swam and a wave of nausea swept through his great body. Quickly he put his head between his knees.

'Faint heart never won fair lady,' he sang weakly. 'I'm off to kiss hands,' and he began to rummage about in his canvas hold-all for a morning suit.

'And I'd like a pony each way on Hello Sailor in the 3.30.' Willing hands replaced the receiver for Her Majesty and she returned to her Morning Coffee.

'How did he strike you, dear, the new fellah-me-lad?' enquired her Consort.

'Terribly excited.'

'He could be an improvement . . . not bloody excuses all the time'. His voice adopted a curious Northern whine. 'It's a Tory plot, your Majesty. It's unscrupulous gnomes, your Majesty. Never his bloody fault, was it?'

'When the New Person kissed hands it was as though someone had laid two cold sardines on my knuckles.'

'No man who can handle a tiller can be wholly bad.'

'I suppose not,' said Her Majesty, from the depths of her *Turf Guide*, wondering idly when the Prime Minister had found time to get to grips with a lady of the Chorus.

There was a knock at the door of the Cabinet Room. The PM softly closed the lid of the piano. Some time, he mused, since this ancient room had resounded to a little Beethoven. 'Come,' he rapped.

Sir Alec entered from another age.

'Hello, sir, good to see you,' said the PM, leaping to his feet and bowing.

'Please,' said Sir Alec, 'you sent for me and here I am – as you will see, ready for anything.' He stretched himself out on the ottoman. 'Ready for anything, Skipper.'

'So you are,' said his leader. For certainly Sir Alec's long khaki shorts and Fair Isle jumper, seaboots and deer-stalker contrasted strangely with his own neat blue pin-stripe.

'Alec,' he said, glancing briefly at his mill-board, 'F.O!'

Sir Alec was on his feet at once. 'You could have phrased my dismissal in a rather more gentlemanly manner,' he snapped, 'or perhaps *you* couldn't.'

He stamped a sea-boot petulantly and began to stalk about the room. Not that he really expected to pick up a spoor but he had found deer in some damned odd places. Not to mention badger.

'I beg your pardon,' said the Prime Minister.

'Badger,' he rapped. Had he not once been savaged in the bath at the Kursal?

'Alec,' said the PM, crawling under the Cabinet Table after him. A thin hand was clamped over his mouth.

'Shush. Shush.' The old hunter's nostrils were quivering excitedly. With a sudden twist of his body and a sickening crack as his head struck the table above him, he froze into the point.

'Alec, I want you to go to the Foreign Office.'

Sir Alec slowly relaxed. His nostrils stilled.

'The big block on the corner? Of course, we were there together.'

The PM looked after him fondly as he left. He had certainly made the right decision there. He put a big green tick on the mill-board.

'Next!' he commanded.

EXTRACT FROM THE MINUTES OF A MEETING OF THE COCKS BALDING BRANCH, WOMEN'S INSTITUTE. 20th JUNE 1970. MRS NISBET (HON. SEC.)

1 The meeting was declared open at 14.15 hours by Lady Foulbeach (Chairman).

2 Lady Foulbeach (Chairman) called upon Mrs

Gifford to give the Institute a Talk on 'Dusting – It's Boons and Bugbears'.

3 Mrs Gifford, after a fascinating preamble on the History of Dusting, (what times those were) was speaking of the Dangers of Feather-Dusting to the Uninitiated when Lady Foulbeach (Chairman) rose a trifle unsteadily and called for Three Hearty Cheers for the Conservative Party's Famous Victory. Mrs Ashburton (Vice-Chairman) seconded the Motion.

4 Lady Foulbeach (Chairman) then said that while she applauded Mr Heath she had reservations about him which we of the Institute might not understand as none of *us* had graced Cheltenham Ladies' College. But, she said, if he could get the prices down (CHEERS) lower the Income Tax (LOUD CHEERS) get the Blackies out (CERTAIN OBSCENITIES) and bring back the birch or something like it (OOS and AHS) he would earn her respect. BUT, and it was a big BUT (one of the biggest BUTS we have had at the Institute) should he fail, she would not hesitate to wield the iron glove.

5 Mrs Benson rose on a point of order and said that WIs were not allowed, it was in the Rules, to talk about Politics or Religion and that the Chairman *was* in no uncertain manner, and anyway she (Mrs Benson) had come to hear a Talk on Dusting.

6 Lady Foulbeach said she apologised but that she had been carried away by the emotion of the previous

evening and that in her opinion Politics and Religion were a deal more interesting than an extremely boring talk on dusting (CHEERS).

7 Mrs Gifford resumed her lecture with some views on 'J Cloths – Yes or No ?' and it must be admitted that it *was* very boring after our first taste of controversy.

The Cabinet was assembling for the first time. To many it was like coming home. The Home Secretary sat down more than weightily in his old seat. God knows who had been in it for the last few years. It felt distinctly damp. The floor about it was stained and worn. Nothing, however, was going to upset him today. Everyone was present and correct, chatting excitedly of the Campaign and the heady days to come. Suddenly the chatter ceased. Ferdy Cocker-Spaniell, AAPPS to the Cabinet, bustled through the door, donnish yet abrasive with the slightly out-of-focus face of the confirmed toper. He put some papers down carefully at the empty head of the table.

'The Prime Minister,' he intoned, and pointed towards the door. The Cabinet rose as one. Sir Alec clapped twice. In he strode, making straight for his seat as though to the manner born. He remained standing, his lively blue eyes scanning his colleagues as if he searched for sail upon some blue horizon.

'I don't suppose many of you thought we'd be sitting here this morning,' he said meaningfully. 'I did. I was always certain. I kept the Faith.' There was a pregnant silence.

'The piano looks jolly good over there,' vouchsafed the Home Secretary.

'Doesn't it look well?' said the Prime Minister, 'and it will be there for some years to come,' he laughed. The ice was broken. A roar of amusement and applause swept round the room. The PM counted ten, then silenced the roar with a palm.

'Sit down, everybody.' There was a clatter of chairs and a low buzz of conversation.

'That's enough.' The PM sat down slowly, then rose again at much the same pace. He was savouring these moments. He spotted Cocker-Spaniell sharpening a ball-point in the corner.

'All right, men, let's make History.' He waited to see that Cocker-Spaniell had captured that. He noted with pleasure that the fellow had shorthand. Not of course that it would be needed, as he spoke very slowly, but it was good to know.

'What are your plans, Skipper?' asked Sir Alec. No one had shown him a Manifesto, and he never watched the Electric Television.

'I think it best if we raise our hands prior to speaking, otherwise it gets out of hand,' rapped the PM. Sir Alec raised a bony finger.

'What are your plans, Skipper?' he enquired further.

The PM stared hard and long at a paper in front of him.

'First of all,' he said at last, 'you will notice that there are no ashtrays. I don't like to see those under me smoking. Is that clear?' The Minister of Agriculture ground a Park Drive into the mauve Wilton with little show of grace. 'Fack Oi,' he mumbled to himself, and turned his mind to muck-spreading and other rustic delights.

'Secondly, you all keep your noses clean, if you follow me.' Sir Alec lowered his finger. 'We want no repetition of what went on under Macmillan. I've got one of our top men at the Yard on to that,' continued the PM, 'so watch it.'

Some members of the Cabinet looked furtively at one another. Some had the decency to blush. Memories are long in Politics.

'Thirdly. I am initiating a New Style of Government. This means Less Government. In many cases No Government at all. People must learn to stand on their own two feet.'

It was unfortunate that Cocker-Spaniell chose this moment to rise. Unsteadily he began to circumvent the cabinet table passing out sheets of Roneo-ed pink paper.

'My plan,' explained the PM. 'The country is going to find I am a completely different bottle of fish to my predecessor. I am going to have no Instant Government here. I am going to have no Government by Television here. I am going to have no midnight snacks with the Unions here. I am going to have a

Think Tank.' And he was gone. The Cabinet
pocketed their copies of the Plan.

'That can cause blindness,' thought the Minister of
Health.

Opposite Number Ten in that great grey building that
houses the Ministry of Works (Catering and Light
Refreshments) is a dark opening to a shabby stone
stair. Were the unwary pedestrian to enter and climb
that stair to the third floor he would find himself outside Room 2033 – the Nerve Centre of a branch of
Scotland Yard so obscure and yet so vital to the
security of the nation that were this same unwary
pedestrian to gain entry to Room 2033 he would instantly be thrust into a large sack and put on the filing
cabinet.

The tall spare man who sprang lithely into Room
2033 at 08.00 hours on Monday the 23rd of July,
deftly throwing his bowler-hat into the waste-paper
basket, was none other than the Head of the Department, Chief Inspector Gerald Hell. A sack twitched
on the filing-cabinet – he whacked it with his *Daily
Mirror*. He felt randy as a badger. He crossed to the
window and looked down into Downing Street. The
PM was just getting into his Princess. Hell looked at
his watch. 'So's Prince Rainier,' he chuckled to himself. 'Hang about, Hell,' he thought, 'no time for
little jokes.' He made a mental note of a bronzed, full-
breasted corker in the small crowd below. His special

brief, outlined to him by the PM the previous evening, was to ensure that no breath of scandal touched the Administration, not like last time. And that little corker could bring down a Government, he thought, given half a chance. Perhaps he ought to pull her in, just to get a feel of the task ahead. He pressed his face to the window to get a better look at her.

'Biggest cock in the Force, him,' said PC Kraggs to his opposite number, as he looked up and across Downing Street at the face at the window. 'Gawd, there's a tale or two I could tell about *him*.' His attention was arrested in no uncertain manner by the disconcerting approach across the road of Miss Adelaide La Perouse.

'Excuse me,' she breathed in husky Australian.

'Anything,' riposted Kraggs gallantly.

'Is that right the Prime Minister's single?' She began to polish the button on his right breast pocket with a white-gloved finger.

Kraggs winked to his colleague over her hat. 'It is rumoured that he is secretly engaged to Brigitte Bardot.'

'Which is why he is so keen to get into the Common Market,' said his colleague, a young fellow from Bude.

'Wish he bloody would,' Kraggs cried. It is not impossible to be a policeman and a Socialist. Adelaide smiled at them both, and undulated away, a bold idea forming in her lovely head.

Up aloft, Chief Inspector Hell wiped steam off the window with his sleeve. *That* would certainly bear closer inspection.

There are fewer livelier minds in the gaudy, romantic, suede-booted, neon-lipped, varicose-brained demi-monde of Advertising than that of Charles 'Cocky' Forbes of Chitt, Forbes and Bogger, and he enjoyed the game. An old friend of Ferdie Cocker-Spaniell's, he had thrown the meat of his experience behind the Tory Campaign. The Prime Minister's long side-burns were an idea that had come to him under the drier at Vidal Sassoons'. He recalled with pleasure the excitement he had felt when after some forty-three lunches, countless meetings and ultimately a week of late-night sessions, they had been accepted by a majority of the then Shadow Cabinet. 'We've got to grab the women of Britain,' he had said, and, by God, they had. There are those who have said 'We shall cut prices at a stroke' bore the Forbes stamp. It did. He had not spent a fruitful fifteen years in the Credibility Abyss for nothing. In his world poorly shredded Hampshire ragwort was Finest Virginia Tobacco, with Virility in every Puff. A Heady Pint of Gutsy Strong Ale might well be a short measure of second-hand water, but suggest with enough conviction that its toxic properties will cause ladies to roll over on their backs and wave their legs in the air and you can sell a million gallons a year. He had and it did.

Selling a Prime Minister had therefore been bacon for breakfast to him. It was he who had suggested the PM took up boating, which enabled him to borrow most successfully ideas he had previously rejected for a campaign promoting Barnacle the Under-arm Deodorant with the Manly Tang of Seaweed.

The Party had been delighted. Ferdie had rung him on the Friday after: 'What would you like? Just name it.'

'Oh, some honorary position like Public Executioner,' he had laughed, thinking no more of it – after all they'd paid him enough.

It had come as some surprise therefore, the following Monday, when his secretary the Divine Sarah had dumped unceremoniously on his desk a length of stout rope secured with a purple ribbon, a large black hood with slits for the eyes, and an illuminated parchment signed by the Home Secretary granting him 'for what it be Worth, and for so Longe as He doth hath Stomache for the Businesse' the post of Public Hangman. And handsome the document now looked, framed above his desk next to his Paul Klee and a photograph of himself and the PM, sideboards and all, enjoying a joke at the boat show.

Back to the business of the day. The Milk Marketing Board was looking for a healthy front for their product and Forbes was idly thumbing through *Spotlight* for a suitable face and measurcment. And there it was. There they both were. He flicked down the switch on his intercom.

'Sarah, love, fix me a date with one Adelaide La Perouse.'

'A million housewives every day, Tear off their knickers and shout "Hooray",' she sang. Forbes smiled. 'I'm just off to my first lunch, sweetie,' he intercommunicated, 'at the Trat.'

'You're absolutely right, Skipper,' said the Foreign Secretary, without moving his lips. 'This is what they want. Like it or not.' The PM handed him a cablegram. Sir Alec laid it on one of the less dusty patches on the mantlepiece and peered at it closely.

'The good Doctor himself,' he mused, studying the signature, first one way and then the other. 'Doctor Vorster went to Glorster in a shower of rain. Ten thousand bazookas? One thousand ground-to-air missiles? Five thousand Pom-Poms?' He smiled at the vaguely familiar face in the mirror. 'They must have bloody enormous grouse on the Veldt.'

'It's worth a pretty penny to us,' said the PM, 'but that is not the main consideration.'

'Of course not.' Sir Alec dropped the cable into the IN tray. 'What is?' He added hurriedly; 'If you don't mind my asking, but it's the type of question I might have to answer.'

The PM did not tell him. He had momentarily withdrawn into himself. He could be away for some time. It was a disconcerting habit but one Sir Alec had become used to, and it allowed him time to think.

'There'll be a bit of a stink, won't there? Not of course in my constituency where they are impervious to the rattle of shot, I mean long-haired weirdoes like the Archbishop of Canterbury and such. It's going to upset a few people.'

'Sod them,' said the PM suddenly.

'Ah, you're back. Hello again. What I mean is you remember all that schemozzle about the Cricket Tour? I remember saying at the time to the Minister of Sport that there's no place for Politics in Sport. Cricket's one thing and Politics is another. I remember in 1943 advocating quite loudly that simply because we were at war with Herr Hitler, that should not in any way be allowed to interfere with the projected tour by a German Cricket side. I received quite short shrift.'

'Our line, Alec, is that we don't want Russkie sneaking around the Cape of Good Hope and up the Solent and playing all kinds of merry hell with Cowes Week while our backs are turned.'

'The swine. We should have finished them off at Sebastopol. I said so at the time. Perhaps I should say so again?'

But the PM was no longer with him. He had returned to his private thoughts and was immersed in a Great Vision.

EXTRACT FROM THE MINUTES OF A MEETING OF THE COCKS BALDING BRANCH, WOMEN'S INSTITUTE. 14th AUGUST 1970. MRS NISBET (HON. SEC.)

1 The meeting was declared open at 16.30 hours by Lady Foulbeach (Chairman).

2 Lady Foulbeach (Chairman) said that instead of the advertised Lantern Lecture by Mrs Sutton-Bishop on a Charabanc Tour through the Weald of Kent and Back, she herself, Lady Foulbeach (Chairman), because we lived in troubled times, was going to ease our burden by reading to us excerpts from *St George Among the Daisies*, a new collection of poems by Mr Enoch Powell.

3 Mrs Sutton-Bishop rose on a point of order and said she had never been so insulted in all her life, yes, she had, but that was another story and involved a former Mayor of Ramsgate.

4 Mrs Benson rose as is her wont and said the comments of Lady Foulbeach (Chairman) and proposed readings smacked of politics and didn't she know the rules, and anyway she had been born in the Weald of Kent and had been looking forward for some weeks to seeing pictures of it.

5 Lady Foulbeach (Chairman) said that she had said it before and would say it again that it was high time the Womens Institutes of Great Britain forgot about the rules and took matters into their own hands. '*St George Among the Daisies* – Poem One,' she read out.

'Had Sophocles been black would he have been as wise as I?

Answer me, Plato, from your lofty plinth,
Had you had piccaninnies wet upon your pale
  Caucasian knee
Would you have been superior as me?'

6   Mrs Benson began to chant 'What about the Weald
of Kent?' and a rather poor picture of a charabanc
was projected onto Lady Foulbeach (Chairman).
Lady Foulbeach (Chairman) then got her paddy up
and began to shout back that what this Great Island
of ours needed was Great Leadership, and we were
very unlikely to get *that* from the silly sailor-boy in
Number Ten at the moment.

7   Mrs Greaves, who has previously never said a word
at any of our get-togethers, then stood up and said
she liked the Prime Minister, that he was a real man,
not like some, and rather sweet in a funny sort of a way.

8   Lady Foulbeach (Chairman) poured scorn on the
unhappy Mrs Greaves and said this was the sort of
wishy-washy thinking that had got a man into
power who was quite prepared to allow all manner
of darkies and the like to remain in the country and
at any moment would be dragging us into the
Common Market and we all knew what that meant.

9   Mrs Bancroft shouted that she had no idea what it
meant but she didn't like the sound of it at all.

10 Lady Foulbeach (Chairman) painted an extremely
ugly picture of a Britain of the Future, not only stiff
with Black People, but running amok with Huns,

Wops, Frogs and Dagoes and all sorts of other foreigners. No Englishwoman would feel safe to walk the streets. Mrs Ashburton (Vice Chairman) and a crawler) said she agreed with every word.

11 The Meeting then broke up in some disorder, but I heard several ladies say that it had been most stimulating, and considerably more fun than a boring old talk about the Weald of Kent, which we'd all heard last year anyway.

Cocker-Spaniell limped down the stairs very slowly. Last night it had all seemed most pleasureable. The cup that cheers? he thought. If a cup cheered now his head would fall off.

The Prime Minister stood in the hall, sniffing.

'What's that appalling smell?'

'It's the dustmen, sir.'

'Is it? Well, get on to County Hall and tell them in future to send us some cleaner dustmen. *Or else*, add.'

'They're on strike, sir.'

'Holding the country to ransom, Cocker-Spaniell,' he snarled.

'I imagine you'll be expected to say a few words to the press about it, sir. Do you want me to rustle something up?'

The Prime Minister was standing rigidly at attention, scarcely breathing. During the lengthy intermission, Cocker-Spaniell tried to assemble his bent mind into

some crude order. Eventually, the shoulders began to move and then the mouth to open and shut.

'*Expected*, did I hear you say ? *Expected* to say a few words ? I do not think that it is the job of Her Majesty's First Minister to think, let alone speak, about . . . dust-men.'

Cocker-Spaniell held his forehead. 'I'll get on to the war-box,' he said.

'No matter what precedents were established by my predecessor, you will hear no more from me on the subject of dustbins, Cocker-Spaniell.'

'No, sir, I'll ask the housekeeper to do something about the pong.'

'I am taking no calls today,' said the PM. 'I am going into the cupboard under the stairs to look at my tackle.'

The Divine Sarah poked her head round the door of Forbes' office, and beamed happily.

'Christ, Cocky, what've you been up to ? There's a right sexpot out here asking for you.'

'Miss La Perouse, isn't it ?' he said. 'The Milk Marketing Board caper, I think. Wheel her in, dear.' Jesus, if she was only half as good as she looked in *Spotlight*. He groaned deeply and the desk began to shift.

Adelaide gave him the full vow-rupturing walk. Forbes waved a greeting and signalled a few pirouettes. He looked her up and down. Lit a pipe and looked

31

her down and up. Had he prodded her with a walking-stick and said 'R' a few times she would not have been in the least surprised.

'Would you moo, please?'

Adelaide did something with her lips that would have sucked the goodness from a three-foot Havana.

'No, love, moo.'

'That's how we moue where I come from,' said Adelaide proudly, for really she had no cause for shame.

'No, love, like a cow.'

Adelaide shrieked with wild laughter.

We can always dub it, Forbes thought to himself. Get Sellers or Danny Kaye. He jotted the names down. He told her his thinking.

'Why not get a bleeding cow?' she laughed. It would certainly cost less, but how do you get a cow into a Studio? He made a further note.

'Do you have any pictures of yourself in a bathing costume?' he asked. To hell with it – 'or less?' he croaked. She looked at him almost sympathetically.

'I brought the real goods with me,' Adelaide murmured, and she tossed her wide-brimmed hat onto his lap. 'Why not put that black bag on, sexy?' she enquired sweetly.

His discovery of the tail clinched it, of course. Just what the Milk Marketing Board was looking for. Sarah couldn't really complain.

*   *   *

The business of the morning had gone most satis-factorily. The PM was highly cheered. 'Motion carried,' he chuckled.

'I very much doubt it,' said the Minister for the Environment. '*They're* on strike now.' He looked at his boots. Perhaps for the last time, he thought. 'Could I use your phone, Prime Minister? I'd better check the level of pollution.'

'Don't forget to put your sixpence into the box beside the phone.'

'No, sir.' He dialled, and asked a few searching questions of his Ministry. With a long face he turned to the PM.

'I'd better get on to the Air Ministry Roof, sir.'

'My God,' cried the Prime Minister, rushing for the stair. 'Is it rising that quickly? Where's my chopper?' He began to run upstairs.

'Sir' called the Minister. 'I only want to see if its going to rain.'

But he could hear the PM aloft barking orders to Cocker-Spaniell to the effect that *Morning Cloud* had better be off Westminster Pier in a nonce or he'd have Cocker-Spaniell's guts for garters. At that moment the lights went out.

Chief Inspector Hell had just turned the lamp full blast into the suspect's face when an aggrieved elec-trician pulled the plug out, plunging the country into Stygian gloom again.

'Sodding Sparks!' he shouted. 'They ought to shoot those sodding electricians. Take 'em out and stick Laser guns up their arseholes, that's what I'd do if I ran this bleeding country. Go on, piss off, you,' he said to the hapless victim of his 24-Hour-Question-and-Answer session. 'And if I see you poofing about in Whitehall again I'll have you for indecent exposure for showing your face in public. And get your hair cut!' he shouted after him. For good measure. The back-lash was long overdue. So was the short-back-and-sides-lash.

He sat on his desk with a mighty sigh. He was tired. He pulled his legs up onto the desk and burrowing his head into a pile of search warrants, fell asleep.

MINUTES OF AN EXTRAORDINARY MEETING OF THE COCKS BALDING WOMEN'S INSTITUTE. MRS NISBET (HON. SEC.)

1 Lady Foulbeach (Chairman) did not even bother to declare the Meeting open, but went straight into her Address. She said she was delighted to see so many present as now was the time to stand up and be counted.

2 Mrs Ashburton (Vice Chairman and a right twit) asked everybody to stand up and be counted.

3 Lady Foulbeach (Chairman) called her all sorts of strange names which Mrs Ashburton (Vice Chairman) seconded.

4 Lady Foulbeach (Chairman) said that the country

was going rapidly to the dogs and that something must be done.

5   Mrs Benson rose and said she was sorry to interrupt but for once she found herself agreeing with Lady Foulbeach (Chairman) and the only remedy she could suggest was a Good War like the last one, as it was the only time the men did anything. Particularly her Bruce, now deceased.

6   Lady Foulbeach (Chairman) said how very true. *Her* late husband had had a Good War, so everyone said, and it had done him a power of good, even if he had given a leg he could ill afford. However that was not, begging Mrs Benson's pardon, the issue now to be faced. Although, of course it *was* very like the Last War.

7   Mrs Benson rose again and said that what with the black-outs and the Army doing the dustbins and the price of everything, she wouldn't be surprised if the Government brought back rationing and clothing coupons and blitzes.

8   And why? continued Lady Foulbeach (Chairman). Because we were in the hands of a ninny and there was only one man who could guide us through the Slough of Despond – Enoch Powell. Now she had nothing against the other members of the Cabinet – nice men trying to do their best – we tend, she added generously, to overlook the sacrifices they make (CHEERS) giving up their directorships and highly remunerative jobs in the City to try and run

35

the country properly – but how *can* they while the *present* Prime Minister is in office? Something must be done. She sat down to a standing ovation. Our first ever.

9 Mrs Greaves said that even she was going off the Prime Minister and that at first she had been more than a little attracted to him. But now what with the price of everything, she did not know. So little had been heard of him since taking office, perhaps he had not been well.

10 Mrs Benson proposed that so enjoyable were these Meetings becoming that she would like to see those silly rules about Politics and Religion thrown out of the window at the Annual Assembly at the Albert Hall. The motion was carried unanimously. I think we are all in for a barrel of fun.

If anyone had the time and the inclination to make such a study, it would be possible (given also the necessary sick mind in a strong head) to compose a guide to the Party Circuit on the same lines as London Transport's map of the Underground. Viz (if you'll pardon the expression) the Circuit has its own Inner Circle which, once boarded, can carry you in only a month or so from just off Eaton Square via the more salubrious parts of Westminster and Regents Park to cocktails at Buck House.

Adelaide La Perouse, using another route recommended by Charles Forbes, boarded the vehicle at Hampstead and within a week of hectic party-going was at a junction off the Kensington High Street, where – had she not been certain of her ultimate destination – she could have branched off to Richmond and obtained the title role in *The Nude Werewolf Howls Again Again*. She was not, however, to be led astray. From High St Ken she moved to a *the dansant* in Smith Square where she danced with Norman St John Stevas (that she did so is wholly irrelevant to the plot, but a fascinating gobbet nonetheless). More relevant, she was invited by a singularly unpleasing Lobby Correspondent to a cocktail party the next evening in a tiny flat in Wilton Place. And there we discover her – such is the natural order of things – packed in with a hundred others all fresh from the tender ministrations of their hairdresser or taxidermist, pressed warmly to the front of Ferdie Cocker-Spaniell's Old Harrovian body. 'I'm a friend of Cocky's,' she said.

'Any friend of Cocky's.' He fell against a bookcase. Must see the quack, he thought, I keep doing this every time I have a couple of bottles of Gordons. My God, he stared into his glass with alarm, there are Tories at the bottom of my Gordons. He had to laugh. 'Any friend of Cocky's' he repeated, although he couldn't for the life of him remember having said it before, 'is a friend of Cocky's.' And he smiled knowingly. 'Hang on,' he gagged, 'eyes down for a full basin,' and with that was gone, with Adelaide in hot pursuit.

Ferdie sat on the bathroom floor towelling himself with the curtain.

'Better, but still useless,' he said. 'I won't know you tomorrow but come and have lunch.'

'Where shall I meet you?' asked Adelaide.

'Got a pencil and paper? I shall dictate. Like our Great Leader! Ho! Ho! Ho! The address is Number Ten . . . got that? Number Ten, Downing, as in Swan Upping, *Downing* Street. It's off Whitehall. Just ask a policeman.'

'Will they let me in?'

He pulled a pile of papers from his pocket. Selecting one, he tried to read it. 'No good.' He handed her the paper. 'Just say . . . whatever it says there to say against whatever day it is tomorrow lunchtime to the fuzz outside.'

Adelaide slipped the paper into her handbag. After all, one never knew.

The Inner Cabinet sat uncomfortably around the set in the Television Room. It used to be the second bathroom but was now the Television Interview Room and contained the only set in Number Ten.

'The honeymoon is over,' said the Prime Minister. 'We cannot expect molly-coddling. There are no visionaries on Panorama.'

'Are we on the right wave-length?' asked Sir Alec, almost a total stranger to the instrument.

'I've no idea,' said the PM. 'It's scarcely within the compass of the duties of Her Majesty's First Minister to fiddle with the knobs on a television set. Get Chataway in to give it a good kick.'

'Good evening,' said Robin Day, and all over the country lonely people cried 'Good evening, Robin' for he is their friend. His smile vanished. The famous mole that squats on Robin Day's forehead above the centre of his inquisitor's glasses, began to burrow into the deep furrows between his eyes and throw up mounds of frowning skin.

'The Quiet Revolution. A Panorama Report. The Quiet Revolution, as we have come to know it, was first mooted at the 1970 Tory Conference at Blackpool by the then Leader of the Opposition – the New Edward Heath as he was proclaimed. Incidentally, the 43rd New Edward Heath to be so proclaimed since they came up with him in the first place. And one of the last. As they were fast running out of him. I hope the Prime Minister will appreciate my little joke.' He hazarded a thin smile. 'Let us first look at the Revolution itself. Over now to Morton Beastquick who has been holed up in the St Stephens Tavern since the Revolution began.'

Morton was pissed as a judge. He was not an ideal choice for Outside Broadcasts. They could contain him to some extent at the Television Centre but he had now been in what he euphemistically referred to as 'the field' for some weeks. But he could rightly claim that he was the BBC's Revolution Specialist and that was good enough for him. By God, he thought, they can hardly complain if you have a nip or two at the end of a hard day at the barricades. Great piles of dustbins and reeking sacks jam-packed with rotting cabbage were surely excuse enough. He staggered through the doors of the snug, his ears still ringing from the dreadful noise of the silent majority. He looked ap at the television. Bloody Robin Day was on the telephone.

'Jesus, Mort, there you are! For Christ's sake, you're ON.' An anxious producer was wetting himself.

No panic. Morton was a professional. With but a second's pause to run his fingers through his bright red hair and hurl a large Bell's down himself, he hawked, spat and prepared to address the nation.

'All is quiet now in Whitehall,' he rasped through his nose, as it has been since George Gale went home. I can still hear the rattle of typewriters in the distance, the occasional pop of a flashlight, and even the odd shot being fired round the Foreign Office. That, however, is reported to be Sir Alec blowing duck to pieces in St James' Park. All in all, I would say that the Revolution is over and merely add that in 35 years of attending Revolutions all over the world I have never known a quieter. Morton Beastquick, where am I?'

He made at once for the bar. It may not have been much but it would mean he could hold his head high in the Off Licence once more. He glanced up at the set again. Day was interviewing some fatly-paid hack in the studio. It was only then he realized that he had not been holding a microphone.

'Well, Robin,' said the fatly-paid hack with a nation at his mercy, 'one associates the Prime Minister with quietness. Indeed I for one feel that he is at his best in moments of total silence. But since June 18th there have admittedly been rumblings in the land. Has the country fallen into the hands of deranged Trappists? Is there anyone at the helm? Is the Ship of State to suffer the same fate as the *Marie Celeste*? These are the anxious and to my mind totally justified queries. Is there anyone in? Hello, Hello. Woo Hoo, we cry. Say something, even if it's only "Go away with your balls-aching questions, this is a New Style of Government and some of us are trying to get some sleep." But answer comes there none.'

'Thank you, Norbert,' said Day, ungratefully, 'and yet it would appear that in true Revolutionary spirit the Tory Party, already aptly named the Suburban Gorillas, have under cover of total blankness, achieved the two main objects of a successful coup. The take-over of the BBC and the neutralising of the Army. Lord Hill, are you the enema within?'

A large military gentleman in a gas mask stared at him strangely. 'I am not Lord Hill, my dear fellow,

I am Major General Briggs, and would you mind most frightfully if I remove my bearskin as it is damnably hot under these lights of yours.'

Robin Day was thumbing his way feverishly through a pile of yellow papers. It in no way disturbed the General, who removed his bearskin and pressed on.

'I thought we were going to get another crack at Johnnie Gippo. Picture if you will my amazement to find myself not on the banks of the Nile that I know so well, as I do the souks and bazaars of old Cairo, but up to my knees in the dungy reaches of Old Mother Thames. It took me some time to persuade the men that Henley was not Port Said. It was the total absence of camel that first roused my suspicions, followed by a wire from the War-Box reading 'For Suez read Sewage'. Of course, most of the chaps are in Belfast or the NAAFI Club, Bad Oynerhausen, so that my tiny detachment are literally up to their eyes in it.'

'The stage was now set,' continued Day, perspiring freely, 'for the Selling of Arms to South Africa. The Attorney-General made a vigorous speech about the Rule of Law and announced that he was contemplating arming Traffic Wardens. The Prime Minister inserted an advertisement in *Exchange and Mart* for a "small, multi-disciplinary central policy review staff in the Cabinet" and received replies from seven flagellants, nineteen voyeurs and a coven of Hat-fetishists in Croydon. The Chancellor took sixpence off the Income Tax so that Sir Arthur Jodrell, the well-known

Banker, would say that he was tough. He also raised the price of school meals, demonstrating courage and vision. In the studio we have the Foreign Secretary.' ('I'm a Recording, explained Sir Alec to the PM).

'Foreign Secretary,' said Day. 'Why Arms to South Africa?' ('I think you're going to enjoy this,' Sir Alec continued to the PM, who was now sitting up on the ottoman, stiff as a board.' 'No,' said the recording of the Foreign Secretary, 'I have been misquoted. We are not selling the Gurkhas to South Africa. I wonder if Mrs Meir would like them? Are Gurkhas Jewish? What I say is this – why don't the Israelis give the Egyptians their balls back and then we can all get on with the game. We don't want a lot of blacks calling the kettle pot. We don't need any advice from these Africans over the port on how to stand up to the oppressor. Remember Munich. On second thoughts, forget it. No, Mr Day, we are British and as we have before so will we stand alone again. That is why we are going to join the Common Market.'

The Inner Cabinet fell into full and frank discussion. They did not hear Hans Koch compare the Prime Minister's *coup* to the merry song of the blue-bearded warbler, harbinger of happy times and much jollity in the spinneys.

They paid no attention when a distinguished Member of the House of Lords was asked who would recognise the New Government and replied that they

43

all looked the same to him. They did not even say 'Goodnight' to Mr Day when he signed off. Their minds were elsewhere. The PM climbed on to a chair to address them.

'My plan,' he announced. 'We call off the Quiet Revolution. We sell these Arms to South Africa. We're booted out of the Commonwealth. Goodbye New Zealand rhubarb, Waltzing Matilda and all that rot and into the Common Market by Tuesday at the latest. Take a letter, Cocker-Spaniell, to Monsewer Pompidou.'

'I'm afraid, sir, that the postmen are now on strike.'

'Then send a frogman.' He could not understand why the Home Secretary found that amusing.

Cocker-Spaniell steadied himself against the bust of Disraeli, he could barely stand and it was not yet lunchtime. The midnight oil had been burnt to nothing composing a grovelling note to Pompidou. That, the weight of many nightcaps on his balding head and the fact that he had had to rise early for drinks with a Saudi-Arabian trade delegation, saki with the Japanese Ambassador, champagne with the TUC and a pre-prandial with a Convention of American lawyers, had left him much the worse for wear.

'Why haven't I had my monthly?' bellowed the PM from the piano.

'It's the postal strike, sir, I'll get Smiths to deliver one.'

'Go yourself, matey. You need the exercise. And get me a *Boating Weekly* as well,'

Ferdie swore at Disraeli and all his successors, particularly the latest. He reeled towards the door, threw it open and made to slam it. Framed in the doorway, however, was a vision of such loveliness that he held everything.

'You asked me to lunch,' said the vision of loveliness. Number Ten had never seen the like. Apart, of course, from brief glimpses of Mrs Thatcher.

'Done,' replied Cocker-Spaniell. 'Come with me, whoever you are.'

The *Yachting Monthly* might never have existed.

Chief Inspector Hell was down his dingy stairs in a flash. This could be it. That bronzed houri again, arm in arm with the man he had long felt was the weak link in the chain. If there's a pisspot in the monastery, throw him out, was an adage tried and true. And if Number Ten was now a monastery, that Cocker-Spaniell was certainly a pisspot. He set off in pursuit along Whitehall.

'It's the backlash!' cried the PM, excitedly, waving his *Evening Standard* aloft. 'Alec, listen to this.'

Sir Alec cocked an ear. It was high time the tide turned.

The PM began to read. 'Seventeen plucky little Hello Girls in Hot Pants parachuted into the City

45

this morning with the latest Time Signal. "Pip pip pip" said plucky little Hello Girl Madge Thompson from Sidcup, Kent, "at the third stroke it will be seven twenty precisely." "This is the spirit that made Britain Great," said a spokesman for the CBI, "the sooner we are in Europe the richer I shall be." What about that?' The PM waved the paper in front of the Foreign Secretary.

'Have we had any reply from Mr Pompadour?' he asked.

'I think,' the PM thought aloud, 'that it's high time I addressed the nation.'

'They'll be jolly pleased,' said Sir Alec.

'Where's Cocker-Spaniell?' And then he remembered.

Scandal. There must be no whiff of scandal. Those were his orders. He was through the swing doors of the London Hilton as the lift gates closed upon his quarry.

'Whore! Bloody whore!' he shouted, and barged his way to the Reception Desk.

'What room has Cocker-Spaniell taken for the afternoon?'

Reception looked slowly up at him. 'He is not to be disturbed, sir, his express instructions.'

'It is imperative that I speak to him.'

'Sorry, sir,' and as Reception bent once more to his task, Hell noticed a ten-pound note sticking from his breast-pocket. Cocker-Spaniell had obviously bought his silence.

Hell banged his fist on the desk.

'Take me to him at once.'

Time was flying by. They could be at it by now. Photographers secreted in the wardrobe. Russian agents in the shower.

'What is your name, sir?'

'My name? You want my name?' Hell panicked. For security reasons he embarked on a pseudonym.

'Ah. Ah. Gorms – ' he started. Inspiration failed him. 'Gorms – mmmmmm,' he finished. He sighed with relief.

'Could you spell that, Mr Gormsmmmmmm?'

Hell felt a cold hand clutch his bowel. Warm hands were prohibitively expensive these days.

'No,' he said, 'and anyway it's none of your business.'

'I was going to send the lad up with a note.'

'Oh,' said Hell 'Ah. 'G.' he began, 'O . . . R . . . M . . . ' he continued, 'S?' he hazarded, and then sprinted for the end, 'D . . U . R . M'.

'I knew a Cyril Gormsdurm once,' remarked Reception with a strange smile. 'Are you, sir, from the Wirral?'

Too much time had been wasted. To Hell with it, he slapped his Warrant Card on the desk. Reception read it slowly.

'I'll see he gets it back, sir,' he whispered urgently. 'I thought nobody could really be called Cocker-

Spaniell, even for the afternoon. Funny, I can usually spot the Fuzz at fifty paces.'

Reception laid his hand on that of Hell.

'Cyril Gormsdurm was a great friend of mine. A truly great friend. Dare one hope it runs in the family?' He waggled his eyebrows.

Hell didn't stop running till he had reached Piccadilly.

'The Prime Minister,' said a disembodied voice, and the screen slowly filled with tanned flesh and white enamel.

'Avast there, mateys. I am the first to admit that the first six months have not gone entirely to plan. They told me that the first six months would be the worst. So what have I done. I have ignored them. If you ignore a thing it tends to go away. Let me illustrate that point with a nautical yarn specially spun for me for this broadcast by Coleman, Prentiss and Nigel, my Valet. When I am in my lovely boat, pissing and totching off the Isle of Wight and a sudden squirrel pops up – I think that should read "squall" but of course one must be prepared for anything on the High Seas – I ignore it. And of course – or off course as we say on *Morning Cleoud* – blast – *Cloud* – in the end it goes away. After one has had a good, long cool look at it, mind you. All that is now behind us. What lies ahead?'

*   *   *

Lady Foulbeach turned away from the set, a look of repugnance on her fine old features. She looked across to Mrs Benson, her old adversary, now seated comfortably on the sofa in the drawingroom of Foulbeach Towers, sipping a glass of the local porto.

'I think we see eye to eye on this matter, Mrs Benson, although I am a trifle taller. We must be up and doing. Strong measures, Mrs Benson, strong measures.'

Lady Foulbeach glanced back at the screen.

'He *is* wearing make-up, you know.'

Mrs Benson, she was happy to see, was not listening. She was totally engrossed in a huge battle-axe that dear Henry had had mounted over the Adam fire-place. She would make a stalwart ally in the business ahead.

The Prime Minister was reaching the point.

'We must make Britain Great again. But heow – blast – how? I have had a vision. I have also heard voices in the garden. Her Majesty's Government has decided that we must with all expedition push through our application to join the Common Market. This is a Great Turning Point in our History.' And as if to illustrate the point he began to go round and round in circles again.

'He's no bloody idea what he's at,' moaned Ferdie Cocker-Spaniell. He lay naked as nature never intended on top of the wardrobe in snorkel and

49

flippers. He had been having a wonderful time until he'd turned the telly on.

'He must have written the bloody thing himself.' He did feel a mild twinge of conscience but he had given them the worst year of his life, and he needed the rest and relaxation. If Miss Adelaide La Perouse could be so described. He would go and make his excuses at the ball that night at Hurlingham. The PM was bound to be in expansive mood after this little triumph.

He heard Adelaide splashing about in the bath.

'I'm ready, love,' she called. He read quickly through the page in front of him. The Congress of the Sperm Whale. Yaroo! He adjusted his snorkel and plunged off the wardrobe with a wild cry.

'The Common Market is a Great . . . Thing' continued the Prime Minister. 'A Great Thing. The Tide of History. The March of Time. All our Yesterdays. The Lost City of Atlantis. The Holy Grail leaps to mind. The Holy Grail leaps to mind. I think the tele-prompter's stuck. Thank you. And if this is a Giant Step for Mankind who better to take it than your friend and mine – Geoffrey Rippon, once Mayor of Surbiton and no stranger to the Crowned Heads of Europe. Like myself a man cast in the mould of heroes. A fine shape for statues. Ask yourselves will my profile not enhance the Commemorative Coins and Stamps ? Oh, I will be a Great Prime Minister yet. I shall achieve what neither Charlemagne nor Napoleon nor Adolf Hitler succeeded in doing. Bringing this once great country to its knees.' (Elgar was gently playing in the background, almost unable to contain himself.) 'Oh,' sang the Prime Minister, 'I shall go down to the sea again . . . '

'For the third time, I hope,' said PC Kraggs, whimsically.

'Who said that?' snapped Hell. There was no answer. 'Right, lads, show's over, you know your positions. Move!' He blew his whistle and his men, in dinner jackets and heavy boots, ran to their posts. Hurlingham was sealed.

Hell turned off the television and ran his eye quickly over the room. This would do admirably. You never knew what you might not pick up at this sort of function. He went to the door. It was locked from the outside. Well, *he* wasn't going to make an exhibition of himself. Frowning deeply, he turned the television on again.

Lady Foulbeach put the key in her handbag. She was taking no chances, even if this was only a reconnaissance. Not with the obnoxious Gerald Hell about.

'I thought it went tremendously well,' said the Prime Minister. 'Quite brilliant,' said a colleague. 'Churchillian,' said another. 'I think it showed who's boss,' said the PM, and ordered a Black Velvet. He looked at his card. 'There's *Always Tomorrow*. Foxtrot. Lady Foulbeach.'

Cocker-Spaniell was at his side.

'I'm sorry I let you down, sir. I collapsed from nervous exhaustion. You were masterly, I thought.'

'Of course I was. I don't need you to tell me that. Where's my bloody *Yachting Monthly*?'

'In my car, sir,' Ferdie lied. The PM grunted.

'Who's this Foulbeach woman?'

'Very big in the Womens Institute, sir.'

'What do I say to her?'

Cocker-Spaniell began to brief him hurriedly.

'Excuse I,' said Adelaide forcefully, and unclipped the PM's large bronzed hands from the white gloves of Lady Foulbeach. 'I could never go home to Brisbane saying I'd missed the chance to dance with the Prime Minister of England, now could I?'

Lady Foulbeach stood pensively. A detective started forward.

'I can handle this,' said the PM and motioned the detective towards Lady Foulbeach. He knew his duty. Grasping Lady Foulbeach in the regulation manner he danced her off backwards into the *melée*

'I knew you wouldn't mind,' breathed Adelaide. After all it was spring, and a young man's fancy . . . but then again, it wasn't spring, he wasn't young and perhaps he didn't fancy it.

'I *do* mind, but I was brought up to grasp the nettle

firmly. An unpleasant incident has been averted due to my shrewd diplomacy. You are a silly little woman.'

'Call me Adelaide,' she mouthed huskily, working her moist lips to the bone. 'You have a gorgeous suntan, really.'

'I like to keep myself in good condition,' The PM was searching desperately for Hell. Where was the bloody man?

'It's so nice to meet a man with a real tan. It's very manly, if you know what I mean. They're all so white over here. Not you, though. You're bronzed and fit – the Outdoor Type, I'd say.'

Where *was* Hell? Rot the man. No matter. Rescue loomed. Cocker-Spaniell. He had taken charge of Lady Foulbeach and the couple swirled towards them at pace. Good for Ferdie! For once.

'Excuse me,' said the PM, but Adelaide had him in a vice-like grip. 'Excuse me.' Struggle seemed useless. He tried to throw her off but she twined herself further about him.

'Why have you never married?' she purred. 'You're a terrible waste.' This was becoming intolerable. Oh, that he was at sea, with a stiff nor' easter whistling through his mizzen, and the salty clean taste of spray upon his lips.

'Get this woman off my back, Cocker-Spaniell,' he whispered urgently.

'At once, sir. Come down, woman. At once.' And he grabbed at Adelaide to no avail. 'We've never met, remember,' he called up to her. Her thighs tightened their hold about the PM's neck.

Photographers were beginning to barge through the dancers. Only one thing for it. He took firm hold of the Prime Minister's hand and began to pull him and his exotic load towards the exit.

'Make way for the Prime Minister!' shouted Cocker-Spaniell. 'This lady has had an attack and at great personal cost the Prime Minister has her in a fireman's lift. Run, sir, Give them air, please. Stretcher-bearers!' he cried. The Prime Minister had worked up a lively pace now and was almost there. Adelaide waved and sang from her perch on his massive shoulders.

'It certainly bears all the symptoms of a fit,' said Lady Foulbeach, who knew her fits. But she was not convinced.

The Prime Minister came to a sudden halt in a small ante-room. Some of Hell's men succeeded in dragging Adelaide down. The PM's collar came away in her strong white teeth.

'The Kiss of Life,' she groaned, 'the Kiss of Life.'

'You heard her, Cocker-Spaniell,' said the PM. 'In you go.'

'I'd better go and deal with the gentlemen of the press, sir, I rather fancy this can all be used to advantage.'

'Leave the respiration to me, sir.' It was Hell, who had finally been released by a couple from Central Office in search of privacy. 'A pretty speech tonight, sir,' he said, bowing.

'Thank you, Hell,' said the PM, and straightening his tie, strode collarless into the ballroom to a standing ovation. Ten minutes, by his count.

Meanwhile, Hell bent to his task. He recognised her at once. The plot thickens, he thought, but I shall play a waiting game. He lowered his moustaches into Adelaide's hot mouth. His hands began to knead her fine chest. A policeman's lot, he hummed, is about to be shot.

MINUTES OF AN AMAZING MEETING OF THE
COCKS BALDING WOMEN'S INSTITUTE — MRS NISBET
(HON. SEC.)

1 In the absence of Lady Foulbeach (Chairman) Mrs Ashburton (Vice Chairman) opened the Meeting and called upon Mrs Willis to demonstrate some of the jams and jellies she has known. Mrs Ashburton said that while her regard for Lady Foulbeach (Chairman) knew no bounds, it was pleasing to her to see the Institute fulfilling the purpose for which God had intended it. For once. There were some murmurs of agreement, but not many I am happy to say.

2 Mrs Willis rose to say that the most important thing she had learnt in a life devoted to jam and jelly was self-confidence. The stronger the will to succeed, she said, the firmer the jelly.

3 Lady Foulbeach (Chairman) entered with Mrs Benson and told Mrs Willis to sit down, silly old

ninny, she had a thing or two to put to the Meeting.

4 Mrs Willis sat down on a point of order and said that it was quite obvious to her that Lady Foulbeach (Chairman) had been imbibing over-freely and that the condition of Mrs Benson was Proof Positive were further Proof needed.

5 Lady Foulbeach (Chairman) said that she and Mrs Benson were merely 'highly excited' having formulated a plan in the Ladies' Only parlour at the Puking Vole not only to arrest the ever-increasing rise in prices (LOUD CHEERS) but also to put an end to the namby-pamby running of the country (WILD CRIES OF 'BRAVO' and 'BULLY FOR YOU, LADY FOULBEACH CHAIRMAN).

6 Mrs Willis rose as a man and said she was going to continue with her dissertation on Jams and Jellies and that no power on earth was going to stop her.

7 Mrs Benson hit Mrs Willis on the head with the back of a large battle-axe.

8 Lady Foulbeach (Chairman) told her to go away with her ridiculous jellies, Lizzie Willis, we are going to assassinate the Prime Minister (UPROAR).

9 There was a wild rush to second the motion, won by Mrs Benson and her battle-axe.

10 The Motion was carried unanimously except for Mrs Ashburton (Vice Chairman and a drip) who abstained and Mrs Willis who voted against, and wanted it put on record that it was the last time she brought her jellies to the Women's Institute, sod them.

11 Mrs Tremlett (88) then asked the Chairman how she intended to carry out this thoroughly laudable deed.

12 Lady Foulbeach (Chairman) said she had a number of ideas fermenting but that she would need a day or two to formulate them. Suffice to say she had made a close study of the Prime Minister and that he presented a massive target (FURTHER CHEERS).

Captain Ralph Wrigley had had a busy day. His allotment was berserk with Old Man's Nuisance. 'Search and Destroy' – that had been the order of the old days. Well, the search was easy enough. There the Nuisance was staring him in the face, from among the caulies and broccoli. He had spent the day destroying. Slash, cut, parry, slash, until his aching back could stand no more. Had he been an infantryman it might have been different, but his thirty-seven years in the Army had been spent in Bomb Disposal. Now he faced a retirement of Weed Disposal. Slash-2-3-cut-2-3. He sat himself down in front of the television with a sigh of relief. He opened his *Radio Times* as he stirred his tea. There was a Great Occasion to be viewed. He enjoyed those. A Lord Mayor's Banquet to welcome to the City a band of Chinese table tennis players. The Prime Minister himself was to greet the sporting orientals. It should prove to be a most pleasurable affair.

The Prime Minister would not have agreed. Not for

him egg foo yung and bamboo shoots. Nor lobster
balls, even if they were the genuine article. Not for
him ping pong, a dull game at which he had never
excelled. More Alec's meat. He had moreover been
seated between Sir Arthur Jodrell and the manager
of these bloody little yellow men, neither of whom had
the remotest interest in the Secrets of the Sea and
both of whom could, as far as he was concerned, get
stuffed.

Captain Wrigley sat bolt upright in his chair. The old
twitch was at work. He threw Illingworth to the floor.

'Down, cat!' he cried, and reached for the telephone.
His hand was shaking and moist. His lip dry. Nine.
Nine. Nine? Nine, that was it. Christ, would they
never answer. He chewed his moustache savagely.

'Police?' At last. 'Police. My name is Captain
Wrigley. Orpington 423. I spent thirty-seven years
in Bomb Disposal and I know my bombs. I am
watching the Lord Mayor's Banquet on television and
can say without fear of contradiction that the Chinaman
seated next to our Prime Minister – ' he glanced
anxiously at the screen, all was still well but for how
much longer? 'That Chinaman, officer, is ticking.'

'Ticking Chinaman,' the Force repeated slowly.
Wrigley could hear his pen squeaking. The fool was
taking notes.

'And whirring,' he shouted, 'and like to go off at
any moment.'

'Point taken,' said the Force, 'I'll see what I can do.'
And he rang off.

Wrigley sat glued to his screen. Seemingly only
seconds had passed before large hands appeared from
beneath the table and seized the whirring Chinaman.
He was gone in a trice as though he had never been.
The PM was oblivious of the drama. The speech was
going extremely well and he was full fathom five.

'I see a Chink in the Bamboo Curtain,' he said.

Chief Inspector Hell cried, 'Take that you Chinee
devil!' and emptied his revolver into the Lord Mayor's
crimson drapes.

It became something of a Diplomatic Unpleasantness.
The Courts ruled that weeding had obviously taken its
toll of Captain Wrigley's faculties and sent him off with
a caution. The Chinese Manager was awarded the OBE.
Apparently the strangeness of the food at the banquet
had played havoc with his sophisticated digestive system
and had been the cause of slight interference in the
Southern Counties, said a BBC spokesman.

Captain Wrigley swore blind that he *was* right and
that the whole thing was being hushed up for reasons
best known to *Them*. His obvious bitterness impressed
Lady Foulbeach who put his name and address in her
diary for future reference. She also telephoned Miss
La Perouse, of all people. A likely team was forming.

*　　　*　　　*

Hell laid *The Times* out carefully on his desk, open
at the letters page, and began to pace about it. It
seemed innocent enough in all conscience. He lit a
Gold Leaf meditatively. There it was half-way down
the second column. Gingerly he drew a large circle
in red crayon around the letter headed 'Threat to PM'.
Probably the work of a crank, he thought to himself,
but best read it.

To the Editor of *The Times* via Phone-a-Letter

Dear Sir,
(Hell was on the telephone at once. 'Put a man on to
one William Rees-Mogg,' he ordered. 'Four foot two,
eyes-blue, Kootchy Kootchy Kootchy Koo, and a
pronounced limp. Pronounced Llimp, as in Llanelly,
owing to a speech defect. I want to know his every
move.')

Dear Sir,
I am ringing to give warning that unless the Prime
Minister has resigned his office pip pip pip blast
these newpence pip by 10 a.m. tomorrow Hello
Hello are you still there? he will be summarily Ring
Ring Hello this is Burnley 273 get off the line you
bloody little man Pip Pip Pip he will be summarily
executed Engineers here I'm afraid we're having a
little trouble with this line would you care to listen
to some music by the GPO Dance Orchestra while

we fix it Certainly not go away The Prime Minister has deceived the Women of Britain and must therefore be gone pip pip pip click whirr whirr.

Hell walked to the window and stared down into the street. All quiet on the Western Front. He made a note, however, to keep a weather eye on Cocker-Spaniell and his Antipodean floosie.

Sir Alec tossed *The Times* back on to the PM's desk.

'Bolsheviks,' he said.

'Alec,' said the Prime Minister, rising thoughtfully, a strange humility in his bearing, 'am I not a patently honest man? Do I not talk straight from the shoulder? I know I am not as other men. Is that so bad a thing in these torrid days? To be a man only moved by Great Events. Prick me and I bleed. I admit I find it difficult to descend into the higgledy-piggledy of everyday affairs, but now there is a Great Vista opening up for us in Europe, and my passions are aroused. Do I strike *you* as cold?'

Sir Alec shivered but said nothing; he had no idea what the man was talking about.

The Prime Minister rushed towards him and grasping him by the lapels dragged him to his feet. Their faces were inches apart. Sir Alec sniffed. Garlic. The trademark of the Marketeer.

'Alec, I am about to emerge as the greatest leader this country has ever known. I shall be huge, powerful, strong. I shall silence my critics with a wave.

Inspire my followers with a song. I shall make the people of Britain jump. Europe will fall at my feet.'

Sir Alec fell at his feet.

'Unless, of course,' he said, 'they bump you off.'

So much effort did Sir Alec put into a smile of encouragement that his glasses fell off.

If the Labour Party has sometimes been over-sensitive to serious criticism, the Tories have never been able to tolerate jokes at their expense. The general feeling at Tory Central Office was that the famous letter to *The Times* was a joke in extremely poor taste. A natural sequel to the affair of the Chinaman. Cocker-Spaniell agreed with their analysis. He was sitting in the back of the Prime Minister's car, quietly briefing him. It was just after lunch on the day his time ran out.

'And after the fête a helicopter is standing by on the roof of the Bexley Regal, sir,' he concluded.

'Should be in Bembridge for cocktails,' replied the PM. 'You know I love Bexley. Do you think I could say that when I die Bexley will be found engraved on my heart?'

'I shouldn't bother, sir. I think "Liking" is quite sufficient in the case of Bexley. They'll be very pleased with that.'

The Prime Minister stamped his great foot petulantly.

'You'd better brief me on the fête.' Cocker-Spaniell knew this mood only too well. He embarked once more on the briefing.

'2-30, open fête. Three-star note, sir, admire bunting. Knitted by local Chairman's eldest daughter. 2.40 approx, inspect Guides and Brownies. Ad-lib walk over to cake-stall – wife of Agent. 2.45, knock Lady Fitz-Splendidly out of bed. I've arranged photographers for this one, sir, I thought it better that sticking a tail on the donkey with Mrs Cliveden-Reach. I hope you agree on that one, sir, anyway it's cheaper. Ten balls for twenty newpence as opposed to only three tails for twenty-five. Also Lady Fitz is always good for a few thou round about Election Time.'

The car swung through the gates. 'Band!' ordered the Bandmaster of Number 2 Company Bexley Boy's Brigade. 'Band! *True Blue* in F Major! A One-Two-One-Two-Forget it.' The car had accelerated round the bend and vanished up the drive.

The Agent's wife was not, strangely enough, at the cake-stall. However a most homely old body had congratulated the PM warmly on his address and presented him with a handsome plum cake, thick with icing and marzipan.

The PM passed the cake to Cocker-Spaniell.

'I know I shall enjoy this,' said the PM, laughing tremendously.

'I'm sure you will, dear,' said the homely old body.

Neatly lettered on the icing were the words – FOR WHAT YOU HAVE DONE FOR THE WOMEN OF BRITAIN. Cocker-Spaniell could not resist a tiny morsel, and

C

quite naturally fell dead at the Prime Minister's feet.

'The Demon Drink, I fear,' said the PM, and strode off in the direction of Lady Fitz and her bed.

Excerpt from *The Times*:

ROYAL YACHT FIRES ON MORNING CLOUD
AMAZING SCENES
from our Boating Correspondent

Last night an Admiralty Spokesman described the shots fired by the Royal Yacht *Britannia* across the bows of *Morning Cloud II*, the Prime Minister's racing boat, as a 'cock-up in communications'.

He said that a strange female voice had signalled the Royal Yacht, purporting to be the Admiral of the Fleet himself from the Battle Room in the basement of the Admiralty. The voice had warned that the *Morning Cloud* was not what it appeared, but was a devilish Russian trick to get near enough to the Royal Yacht for skin-divers to attach limpet mines to *Britannia's* bottom. 'Her Majesty,' said a Palace spokesman, 'had been most upset by the incident and had immediately sent a crate of Seven-Up to the PM on his boat.'

'I don't think Women's Institutes are quite me,' said Adelaide. Lady Foulbeach allowed herself a smile. She was not going to be disappointed for a third time.

'More tea?' she enquired. Adelaide walked to the

french windows and looked towards the lake where the gardener was wrestling manfully with some monster water-weed.

'No thanks, love' she said. The water-weed seemed to be gaining the upper hand. The gardener was up to his waist in water and beginning to thresh about.

'You may wonder, Miss La Perouse, why I asked you here in the first place. The fact of the matter is that I remembered you from the 1st Birthday Ball at Hurlingham.'

'Now I remember you,' said Adelaide. Could she ever forget that look?

'That is all forgotten,' murmured Lady Foulbeach. The gardener was now hacking about him with a pair of shears. To little avail.

'I thought the Prime Minister took more than a little notice of you. And you of he. I felt I detected a glimmer between you. A charge, so to speak, of electricity.'

'No chance,' sighed Adelaide. No man treated *her* like that.

'Oh, dear,' said Lady Foulbeach, she was to be disappointed again unless Polly did her stuff.

'I stand a lot more chance with that randy copper,' said Adelaide, 'with his French Kiss of Life.'

Lady Foulbeach stood up suddenly. Three dogs fell into the fireplace. This was too good to be true.

'Gerald Hell?' she cried, moving gracefully but at pace to the windows. 'We know all about his little tricks.'

Adelaide giggled: 'Has the Long Arm of the Law been up your Mary Quant?'

Lady Foulbeach smiled and sipped her tea. Adelaide thought it was time she drew her hostess' attention to the plight of her gardener, who was now up to his neck in weedy lake, and clearly doomed.

Captain Wrigley (for it was he supplementing his paltry pension with Thursdays devoted to the Foulbeach weeds) was going under for the second time.

It was quite true – your life does flash before you. Only, he was learning, in expurgated form, in rotten colour and with very poor sound. Under he went again. It only needed Eamonn Andrews and his horrid book. Where had he got to? 1967. Wrigley in Aden. Yes, there he was blowing up some Arabs. There again leaping out of the way of Mad Mitch mounted on a piper. No mention however of Abashag, the Sweetheart of the Forces. 1968. Pirbright. 1969. Belfast in black and white. 1970. The end was nigh. At the hands of water-weeds or no, he would die like a soldier. No, he wouldn't. He was being dragged from the lake by lithe young arms. He could hear dimly the click of shears and feel the water-weed's grip loosening on his neck.

'Bloody tough, these water-weeds,' said a female voice.

'That's his arm,' cautioned a younger, huskier voice.

'Captain Wrigley. Captain Wrigley.' Both voices now. He tried to stand.

'Oh, do be careful now.' Lady Foulbeach took him to her tweedy bosom. 'It's all my fault. I should have warned you. They took poor Henry, you know, my late husband.'

Captain Wrigley sank to the grass. 1971. Saves life of Prime Minister. The Case of the Whirring Chinaman. No thanks. No decoration. Not even a postal card or an invitation to the House for tea.

'The shit,' he said out loud. 'The shit!' And then being an Officer and a Gentleman, he apologised profusely to the ladies.

'Not at all,' said Lady Foulbeach and turned to Adelaide, who was preparing to apply some of the art of respiration that she had learnt at the slobbering lips of Chief Inspector Hell to the recumbent Captain.

'Captain Wrigley is deeply aggrieved at the treatment he has received at the hands of the Government,' explained Lady Foulbeach.

'Tories or no,' bubbled the Captain. 'Rot their guts.'

'Captain Wrigley,' continued m'Lady, imperturbably, 'is going to blow up the Prime Minister for me, aren't you . . . Ralph?' She glanced at her watch. 'That is, if Polly boobs.'

Captain Wrigley could not answer. His mouth was full although Adelaide's sharp intake of breath had cured him instantly. He decided however to lie low and let the time of his life flash before him.

The Cabinet was keeping a respectful silence. Cocker-

Spaniell had been a decent enough sort, and food-poisoning was a wretched way to go. They all wished that they could have got to the funeral.

'PM's late,' said the Home Secretary.

Then they heard him slowly descending the stairs.

'It will have hit him hard,' said Industry. 'They were like that,' and he gestured vaguely with a biro.

Suddenly from just outside the door came a wild cry: 'Mr Christian! Mr Christian!'

The Minister for Social Services shifted uneasily. He hoped the PM was not in one of his tasteless moods.

The PM entered slowly, his face flushed under the tan. He stood expectantly. A low titter began to run about the room. Soon it became a roar of merriment. The PM had a parrot seated on his shoulder. A smile began to course his rosy face. His lips trembled like mating carp. Slowly they parted revealing his splendid teeth – the parrot, a knowing bird, dug in. It tightened its grip more firmly on the PM's shoulder and as the shoulder began to heave and tremble with his booming laughter, the bird swayed to and fro squawking, 'Man the Boats!' How they laughed. Tears coursed down faces that had never wept. Even Sir Alec rolled upon the floor clutching his waistcoat.

The laughter stopped as suddenly as it had started. The PM's face had set once more as though his mouth had fainted.

'I have just been presented with this splendid bird

by the WI,' he said. 'Now to the business of the day. I am personally going to speak to Pompidou. Such a confrontation calls for Greatness. No disrespect intended, Geoffrey.'

The Chancellor was slowly creeping towards him along the Cabinet Table.

'Don't move an inch, Prime Minister,' he whispered hoarsely. The parrot eyed him suspiciously. With a sudden dart the Chancellor, a keen ornithologist and tough and wiry as that noted political animal the ferret, was at the bird's throat. A long and vicious struggle then ensued. Members of the Cabinet flew hither and thither, as did the terrified parrot. Finally it was Sir Alec, with a sixth sense honed to a nicety on the grouse-moors, who downed the bird with a poker.

The Chancellor turned the corpse over with his foot.

'As I thought, Prime Minister. This is no ordinary parrot. This is a Malawi Cockatoo, a man-eater with vicious poison in its beak. One nibble at your ear, sir, and we would have been without your vigorous leadership.'

'Not,' the Chancellor continued under his breath, 'that there are not plenty more of you where you came from.' It was a remark that Sir Alec half heard but was not to understand for some days yet.

Security was immediately strengthened at Number Ten. Armed police, under the direct command of Chief Inspector Hell, roamed the garden. Hell himself was taut with apprehension. That very

evening in blind panic, seeing a strange object moving slowly towards him across the lawn, he found himself drowning Lionel, Stanley Baldwin's favourite tortoise, in the downstairs bidet.

Lady Foulbeach turned off the nine o'clock news. Polly had obviously failed. She turned to Captain Wrigley, ensconced with Adelaide and Mrs Benson on the sofa.

'Well, Ralph, the ball's in your court.'

The Captain chuckled. 'Ironic that you should say that, Lady F, for while in my time I have housed bombs in old Duraglit tins, bottles, lavatory cisterns, even hats, I had never till you just spoke thought of casing one in a tennis-ball.'

'Is it possible?' enquired Lady Foulbeach. She was a jump ahead of the others. On the cover of her *Radio Times* was excited notice of Wimbledon.

'Oh, my word, yes,' the Captain replied, 'anything's possible in my line of business. The problem is always delivery. How to make sure, for instance, that the hat is on the right head.'

'I used to know Peter West,' said Lady F, 'but I cannot imagine for a moment that he would be a party to a venture of this nature.'

'Thud,' said Adelaide, quietly. She took the Captain's red face in her hands. 'You rig up a tennis ball, Cap'n, and I'll fix delivery.' She started for the door.

*   *   *

The Prime Minister looked up from the piano with a smile.

'Ah, Home Secretary,' he said, 'pull up a few chairs and make yourself comfortable.' He played a few bars of *Tipperary*. 'Home Secretary, I've been having a few words with the Lord Chancellor, and he suggested that I put it to you. It struck me that all these attempts on my life, we must arm ourselves with the Ultimate Deterrent.'

The Home Secretary tussled with nightmareish visions of the Bomb being dropped on South Kensington.

'We must restore hanging.'

'We'll never get it through the House.' He thought of making some mild joke about employing the guillotine and pleasing Pompidou no end, but decided against it.

'Sod the House,' said the PM. 'I want hanging back.'

'I'll go and see what I can do,' said the Home Secretary.

WIMBLEDON MEN'S SEMI-FINALS
AMAZING SCENES
From Our Tennis Correspondent

In the first semi-final of the day Errol 'Thud' Miller threw away the first two sets against Ken Rosewall with the most eccentric display of lobbing I have ever witnessed in all my years at the Centre Court. I have always been at pains to point out that Miller is to my mind currently the finest exponent of the lob in the world, but he was far off the mark today. In the first game two of his lobs bounced off the forehead of the Duchess of Kent as she sat in the Royal Box and a third narrowly missed the Prime Minister who was seated some three or four seats away. Ten times in all in the first five games Miller lofted balls into the Royal Box, one concussing a Lady-in-Waiting, Lady Celia Mottworth-Glew, and another striking the Persian Ambassador in the eye.

Obviously shaken by this barrage of balls the Royal Party left. The Prime Minister remained, however, to be the victim as it transpired of the most extraordinary event of the afternoon. Miller, set-point down on his own service, suddenly turned and struck both serves straight at the Royal Box. One knocked Viscountess Tooting's hat off and the other lodged in the Prime Minister's mouth.

The Prime Minister then also left Wimbledon. The umpire, quite rightly in my view, remonstrated with Miller, who went on to win 0-6, 0-6, 9-7, 8-6, 6-3.

'Thud' Miller once again rolled off the splendid front of Adelaide La Perouse and apologising profusely said that he must keep in reasonable nick for the finals.

'And I'm sorry about yesterday, love, God knows I tried. I couldn't find the right ball.'

'It had a bloody great red blob on it,' Adelaide complained, but she had to admit that he'd tried.

75

'Will you marry me like you promised?' he leant over her with a smile.

'Oh. Thud, don't be a twit, I never was going to anyway.' She turned away from him and buried her head in the pillow.

'Thud' Miller wandered towards the basement window and gazed upwards at the heavens.

'Dear God!' he said loudly. PC Kraggs beamed back at him from the pavement. 'Wrong first time,' he jested merrily. 'Have you by chance, sir, one Miss Adelaide La Perouse about you?' He pulled a warrant from his uniform pocket and waved it in the direction of Thud. Miller nodded.

'Who is it darling?' Adelaide called from the bed.

'The fuzz,' he replied sadly.

She was out of the bed in a flash and delving in her handbag. 'Tell Lady Foulbeach – she's in the book – I'll keep Hell occupied if she wants to get in to Number Ten tomorrow.' She produced from her bag the sheet of paper Ferdie Cocker-Spaniell had given her in his late lamented cups, all those months ago. 'That's how she gets in,' she said.

There was a knock on the door.

'Open up in the name of the Law,' said PC Kraggs.

'I'll come quietly,' she called.

'Oh, come noisily,' laughed PC Kraggs, 'and I can put the boot in.'

'If I do this, will you marry me?' asked Thud.

'Of course, I will,' she lied again, kissed him hotly

on the lips and, pausing only to pick up a large
canvas bag in the corner, walked purposefully out of
the door into the waiting arms of PC Kraggs.

MINUTES OF THE FINAL MEETING OF THE COCKS
BALDING WOMEN'S INSTITUTE. MRS NISBET (HON. SEC.)

1 A vast crowd applauded Lady Foulbeach (Chairman) hysterically as she mounted the podium.
2 Lady Foulbeach (Chairman) said that she would be
brief. She apologised to the Meeting for not having
brought the bacon home sooner (SYMPATHETIC
CHEERS). But tomorrow with the help of our brave
little cousin from so very far away, another Con-
tinent, another Hemisphere, she and Mrs Benson
would succeed.
3 I, Mrs Nisbet (Hon. Sec.) rose and weeping profusely wished them all the luck in the world. It was
a most emotional occasion. I formally thanked
Lady Foulbeach (Chairman) on behalf of all present
for all she had done for the Womens Institute. It
had certainly perked up a lot since she had taken
over the Chairmanship. She had made us proud
to be Women again and a power in the land. I then
removed my woolly vest and set fire to it. A
gesture taken up by all present.
4 Lady Foulbeach (Chairman) obviously deeply
moved by our tribute made her way out of the
smoke-filled Hall to a tumultuous reception.

5   I phoned for the Fire Brigade as Mrs Harris'
undergarments had got out of control in a corner.

Radio-Television Francais' leading Floor Manager, and
didn't he know it, bent towards the perspiring British
Prime Minister. 'Are you ready?' he enquired.

'Oui,' said the True European.

'Ah,' said the Floor Manager, observing the damp-
ness, 'le make-up?'

'Quoi?' said the PM.

'Make-up,' the Floor Manager quickly translated.

'Oui, un peu de poudre sur ma tete, s'il vous plait.'
A tiny lady ministered to his brow.

'All right, settle down in the studio,' the Floor
Manager bellowed in English, his own little tribute.
He began to count down. The Prime Minister
cleared the frog from his throat. Better that than a
toad in the hole. He allowed himself a little joke. The
Floor Manager made an intensely Gallic gesture in
his direction and he was alone with a million French-
men.

'Allo, 'allo. Bonsoir, la France. Mesdames,
Messieurs, faites vos jeux sans frontières. Je vous
addresse ce soir au sujet de notre entrée dans le ou la
March Commune. Zut, alors. Pendant sept cent
années nous avons eu la guerre avec vous. Et toujours
pour nous la Victoire.

'Pendant sept cent années nous n'avons pas vous
aimé, les Grenouilles.

'Pendant sept cent années nous avons dit, "Les wogs commencent à Calais."

'Pendant sept cent années nous avons gagné toujours l'Européen Tasse de Football.

'Maintenant tout ca, c'est oublié. Laissez-moi illuminer cette idée avec un propisition nautique. Quand je suis dans mon bateau sur la mer insouciante et tout de suite un minstrel arrive, peutetre c'est un mistral, mais sur la mer qu'est-ce que c'est que ca, que faire, eh? Je l'ignore et il disparut. Aussi avec l'Histoire. Maintenant nous voulons entrer l'Europe. Ou sont mes Entero-Vioforms? Ho ho ho. Ma petite blague.

'Adieu, Nouvelle Zealand, votre beurre et votre fromage.

'Adieu, les Indes de l'Ouest, et votre sucre, le nom de plume de ma tante.

'Adieu, Australie, maintenant c'est 'Allo l'Europe. Dans mon coeur, je suis Européen, comme vous pouvez entendre. Bonsoir, mes amis.'

'Will it affect my standing?' said Her Majesty, turning sourly from the set.

'Not,' said her Consort, 'if you take a little water with it.'

Personally he had nothing against the Common Market, as long as we didn't join the bugger.

'Why didn't we insist they all joined the Empire?' asked Captain Wrigley. He had always thought of France as an unruly part of East Kent.

'I'll run over the plan again,' said Lady Foulbeach. 'Mrs Benson opens fire with her Lee-Enfield .303 from an upper window here,' and she pointed to a map of Downing Street on her lap, 'in an empty office in the Ministry of Works. If she misses, she signals so with the call of a widgeon, which I know you can do, Dorothy, as I have enjoyed it so often at our WI Musical Soirées. On hearing it, I enter Number Ten, using the password Miss La Perouse has so nobly provided and finish the business with the Captain's Sten Gun. If I also fail, our last resort is Ralph himself with one of his splendid bombs.' She rose majestically and raised her sherry.

'I would like to propose a toast,' she announced. 'May Dame Fortune smile on our endeavours.'

'Amen,' said the Captain, not usually a religious man, and downed his enormous brandy in one.

'Well,' said the Prime Minister to the Foreign Secretary, 'we're *in*. Did you see my broadcast? I thought it went terribly well. All the technicians were foreign, you know.'

Sir Alec had watched the programme, and if much of it had passed him by, he had at least caught the gist. Quite a severe attack of it, in fact.

'Monsewer Pompidou was gracious enough to say that no man would have dared to do what I did unless he possessed, I think I have the phrase aright, "folie de grandeur." He, I think, recognises greatness.'

*   *   *

Excerpt from that day's *Evening Standard*:

WIMBLEDON EXPLOSION
AMAZING SCENES
From Our Tennis Correspondent

Errol 'Thud' Miller was involved in another extra-ordinary incident today in the Final of the Men's Singles. Yesterday, it will be remembered, he surprised spectators with his consistent lobbing into the Royal Box. Today, having served an Ace to take the first game from Rod Laver, he was seen to put the second ball in his trouser pocket, and then as he walked towards the Umpire's chair, to go up in an enormous explosion. Nothing remained of the Number 4 Seed except a deep hole between the tramlines. The umpire Mr Norris from Beckenham told me afterwards that British umpires are the best in the world. And in all his experience he had never seen the like. 'I have been an Umpire now for seventy-two – or is it twenty-seven or possibly forty-three – years. I'm sorry I've never had a head for figures.'

Adelaide La Perouse was ushered unceremoniously into Room 2033. Hell looked up from his desk and crushed a Gold Leaf into his cardboard coffee cup.

'OK, girls, you can piss off,' he said to the police-women in attendance. One threw Adelaide's sack on to the desk.

'That's all she had with her,' she said, and they left

Chief Inspector Hell to his inquisition. Hell leered at her. She was dressed in a diaphanous pink negligée.

'We'll try not to keep you out of bed longer than needs be,' he tittered. He pushed a cigarette pack towards her.

'Smoke?' he said, taking one himself. She demurred.

'Let's do this the easy way.' Hell sat back. 'You tell me what's up, and who's up to it, and I'll send you home in a nice car with the lovely Kraggs.' He smiled at her. 'Funny how two of your boy-friends have come to sticky ends or perhaps it was a coincidence, and I'm just too suspicious by nature. Either way it looks like a nice 2-Centre Package Tour – ten years in Holloway and the rest of your life in Botany Bay.'

'Are you a married man?' asked Adelaide, making plans.

'No,' said Hell, 'but nothing you can say will shock me, I promise. Let's start at the beginning, eh?' He turned to the window and checked on Downing Street. It was still there. He pulled down the tatty blind and turned on his favourite lamp.

'What, for instance, do you do to entertain the troops?'

'I'm a *danseuse*,' replied Adelaide.

'A stripper?' said Hell, jotting it down with a trembling hand.

'I prefer to be called a *danseuse*,' retorted La Perouse. She bent down in a lively manner and picked up her bag of belongings.

'Would you like to check on what I do?' Hell rose slowly.

'No peeping,' she said, and began to do mysterious things under her negligée with objects from her sack. He brushed past her and rammed home the bolt on the door. Did he detect a scuffling sound outside in the corridor? He listened keenly but silence reigned. When he turned Adelaide stood in the bright light of his lamp, her negligée at her feet. From shoulders to floor, she was covered in tiny furry bears.

'Stuffed koalas,' she said. 'Real ones don't travel.'

'Of course not,' said Hell.

'It's a pity, 'cos I use real ones at home and they go down a treat. They jump off me and up gum trees in the wings.'

Hell was gaping at her nether regions.

'That's a platypus,' she laughed. 'She's real, aren't you, Nellie? Have you got a bucket of water?'

Hell, awash with lust, began to fill the waste-paper basket from the tap.

Mrs Benson, heavily disguised as a Kleenaphone lady, slipped into Room 2032. Quickly she made for the window, and began to unpack what the casual observer would have mistaken for fishing tackle but which was in truth her dear deceased's Lee-Enfield. She perched on a desk and waited.

The PM put down his lemonade thoughtfully.

'Cut prices at a stroke?' he said.

The Foreign Secretary climbed langorously on to the Cabinet table. 'That's what you said, Skipper. Of course, you were misquoted.'

'But that's what all the fuss is about,' the Chancellor interposed.

'What fuss?' bellowed the PM. The Chancellor walked to the window and gestured to the street. A number of ladies outside gestured back. A large number of them, waving placards and banners.

'Did I say we'd cut prices *at a stroke?*' the PM was incredulous.

The din in the street was increasing. They were chanting 'Prices down!' and 'OUT! OUT! OUT!'

'Shall I phone the Riot Squad?' asked the Chancellor nervously.

The PM nodded. 'And get that fellow Forbes, the advertising man.'

Hell was soggy with pleasure. To Adelaide's not unmusical rendition of *Waltzing Mathilda*, and as a result of some extraordinarily sinuous movements, most of the cuddly little bears had been shed. She was going to make him sweat over the last few and the platypus.

'Up jumped a jumbuck' she sang, and Hell began to jerk uncontrollably.

'It's quite simple,' said the Prime Minister. Forbes sat uncomfortably, a puzzled frown on his face. He pulled out a Burma Cheroot and put it away again.

'I could have said, for instance, cut braces at a stroke. It's not my department though, we need a play on words, you see, and that's where you come in.'

Forbes thought for a moment.

The Foreign Secretary suddenly cried, 'Dutch vice is an utter joke.' The Prime Minister shook his head.

'We can't afford to upset the Netherlands.'

There was a crescendo in the disturbance without. Mounted policemen had arrived.

The Premier's eyebrows knitted, 'Come along. Forbes, you're meant to be so clever.'

'First prize,' piped the Chancellor, 'is but a poke.'

There was a general murmur of dissent.

Forbes' mind was a total blank. 'How nice is an artichoke,' had occurred to him, but he'd used it before extensively in a campaign.

The platypus, a professional to its webbed boots, heard its cue and plunged with exquisite grace into the water-filled basket. Adelaide was revealed in all her splendour. Hell was not made of stone. And after all, her tail was wagging. Casting aside his jacket and wet shirt in one grotesque shudder he was over the desk like a berserk lascar. Adelaide threw herself backwards to the floor.

'It is a far, far better thing I do . . . ' she thought. 'Oh, dear,' she further ruminated as the full weight of the Law came down on her like a ton of bricks, 'I have done far, far, better things.'

Mrs Benson had been waiting eagerly for the sound of revelry next door. It meant Hell was fully occupied. She eased the bolt and fired twice.

Two .303 bullets smacked into the oak panelling beside the Foreign Secretary's ear. Chips of oak spat into his gin. Sir Alec removed them singly with staccato jabs of a bony finger.

'These death-watch beetle will outlive us all,' he said, banging the panelling with his fist. 'When I was here previously, and very briefly, Elizabeth swore she could hear them laughing in the woodwork. I said that it was probably the ghost of Clement Attlee and left it at that. He walks, you know.'

His audience was white-faced and shaking.

'I'm sorry I mentioned it,' said Sir Alec. 'Really he's a most benign spirit, we used to have midnight chats while he flitted.'

Above the noise of horse and woman doing battle outside came a weird hooting.

'That's no widgeon,' said the Chancellor who, as has been mentioned, knew his Ornithology.

Lady Foulbeach almost fell into the hall of Number Ten. 'The captains and kings depart,' she had screamed to the policemen at the door and PC Kraggs had flung the door open for her. Clasping the sten-gun firmly to her she burst into the Cabinet Room, and emptied the weapon into the ample front of the Prime Minister. With an agility that belied her ears she was through the Conservatory and off across the garden before he had fallen backwards into the piano. The lid crashed down on his recumbent form. 'I'd try the Kiss of Life,' said the Chancellor, 'but not just before Lunch.'

Sir Alec wept noisily. 'Poor fellow. Gorn. Gorn. Gorn.' They'd probably want him to take up the reins of office again. Would he never get any rest?

Outside in Downing Street the horses and the women had stilled at the first shots. Only pressmen and photographers were moving at speed towards the door of Number Ten.

The Chancellor grabbed Forbes. There was little time to act. 'Come with me!' he cried and led the startled Forbes upstairs towards the attic.

Captain Wrigley knelt in prayer on the pavement outside. He was not a little surprised to find Lady Foulbeach breathing heavily at his side.

'They'll never look for me here,' she whispered, 'I got him.' The Captain raised a thumb.

A limp and naked Hell stood in the Cabinet Room. 'Nobody leaves this room,' he said.

'Everyone has,' said the Foreign Secretary, drying his eyes.

'They always return to the scene of the crime,' said Hell and sat down to wait.

'Take its legs,' said the Chancellor. Forbes obliged. He had selected at the Chancellor's behest the most life-like of the many dummies that filled the tiny room.

'Now downstairs,' ordered the Chancellor.

This was a precaution he had taken when he had been Chairman of the Party. He had used them to advantage before.

'Hang on,' said Forbes, dropping the stiff legs. 'That one at the back there, I hadn't seen it before, with the grim look. I mean . . . ' He pointed to the head that laughed back at him from between the Chancellor's knees. 'I mean that's not . . . suitable really, is it ?'

'No time. No time,' said the Chancellor urgently. 'For God's sake, downstairs fast.'

Lady Foulbeach and the Captain knelt together. Downing Street was now thick with journalists eager for news.

Suddenly a naked Adelaide slipped between them.

'Lend us your coat,' she whispered. The Captain wrapped her in his worn Burberry.

'Bravo, Adelaide,' Lady Foulbeach murmured softly.

At that moment the door of Number Ten began

slowly to open. The throng pressed forward. Already some flags in Whitehall were at half-mast. The Old-Boy Net had scooped the world.

The Prime Minister, stiff and uncompromising, was framed in the doorway, arm uplifted. There were some cheers and rumblings of disappointment.

Lady Foulbeach gasped. It was unbelievable.

'Ralph, your bomb,' He passed her the lethal container. She hurled it in the direction of the Prime Minister. A direct hit. There was no doubt this time.

As the smoke cleared there was no sign of the late Premier. Save for a few pieces of blue serge hanging sadly from the railings.

'I shall now give myself up,' said Lady Foulbeach and wishing her two accomplices a fond farewell went to join Mrs Benson in the stout grip of PC Kraggs.

Some months had passed. Rumour was still wild in the streets. No official announcement concerning the fate of the PM had been issued. The country was being run by a caretaker Government. If it wasn't him it was the gardener, another incompetent. However, in that morning's papers, it was announced that there would be a Prime Ministerial Broadcast to the Nation at night.

Forbes turned on the television from the switchboard beside his enormous yak-skin covered bed. Even on his wedding night he had to check the product. Adelaide pressed herself closer to him.

She blew in his ear, but she knew she must wait.

The screen darkened.

'There now follows a special Prime Ministerial Broadcast. The Prime Minister.'

Once again the screen darkened.

An expectant hush hung over the land.

Then a familiar face hove into view. Forbes heard Adelaide breathe in sharply.

'He's dead,' she whispered hoarsely. 'He's dead, I saw Lady F. He was shot. And then blown to pieces. He must be a Recording.'

'No,' said Forbes grimly, 'he's Live.' She had never seen him as angry as this. He picked up the red telephone. In a voice icy with menace he asked for Lulubelle.

'Lulubelle,' he rasped, 'That's the bloody Mark VII for Christ's sake. We'd thrown that one out. Look at the bloody lips for God's sake, they're not even in bloody synch.'

Adelaide heard a low urgent voice speaking quickly and apologetically at the other end.

Forbes leapt out of bed white with rage.

'I don't care if the whole bloody Central Office, the whole bloody Cabinet, the CBI, the entire bloody membership of Boodle's and White's thought the Mark IX looked more sincere. I said Mark sodding VII and Mark sodding VII it is. Get that thing off.'

He cupped his hand over the mouth-piece turned to his wife.

'I've spent four bloody months twenty-four hours a day working on that thing's bloody image and they do this to me.'

There was equal anger spluttering from the other end of the line. The PM's voice boomed on. His remarkable escape. The marvels of British plastic surgery. That he had been up and about on the third day. All good stuff and a very fair facsimile. Fair enough anyway.

'I don't give a stuff,' shouted Forbes down the telephone.

'Anyway, love, you won't have to do any hanging,' said Adelaide, soothingly, 'I know you weren't looking forward to it.'

Forbes didn't hear her.

'Look here,' he screamed at Lulubelle, whoever he might be, 'WHO'S IN CHARGE OF THIS FUCKING COUNTRY ANYWAY ?'

Epilogue Part II

Through a veil of tears Mr Justice Trigg watched dear Alice sinking majestically from his view into the depths of the Old Bailey. He rose slowly to his feet. To those who knew him well he would have seemed more unsteady on his feet than was usual even after a heavy luncheon at the Wig and Pen. If so it was only that in his imagination he was steadying himself once more on the bow of a neatly varnished punt in the shade of a friendly willow on the Henley Reach. The punt heaved again beneath him as he lurched towards her – 'Alice, oh, Alice,' he had groaned, abandoning his ukelele and boater to the mercies of an adjacent swan. She had lain there like a meringue. Stiff white linen with a delicious filling of soft, creamy skin. Oh, he had eaten his fill of meringue that sunny afternoon over half a century ago.

'M'lud. M'lud.' An anxious Clerk of the Court was shaking him. A note was pressed into his hand. He read it with precision. A smile lit his wizened purple features.

'Alice! Alice!' he cried, waving the note.

She reappeared from the basement, and studied him anxiously.

'Courage, Nipper, I knew what my fate would be.'

'No, you didn't you gorgeous beast!' he called. 'You didn't do it! In my hands I hold a piece of Pardon. Signed by the Queen herself. I sentence you to be Mrs Trigg as long as I shall last.'

'Cut down on the Old Crusty, Nipper, and I'm yours,' she laughed.

'Done,' was his merry response, and the whole Court began to sing happily.

Epilogue Part III

Police Constable Hell looked apprehensive as the Author finished reading the last grubby sheet of foolscap, and tentatively put it back with the rest in Hell's shopping basket.

'It's unbelievable,' said the Author, shaking his magnificient head.

'I have the proof here,' said Hell, pushing forward a nasty paper bag. The Author peered into it. There were pieces of blue serge and scorched pink rubber.

'And here,' said Hell, producing from his tunic a poorly stuffed koala bear.

'Do you mean to say . . .' The Author was incredulous, . . . 'that the country is in the hands of unscrupulous twisters ?'

'Yes,' said Hell. 'Scouts' Honour.'

The Author stared long and hard at the shopping-basket. Is it fact ? he thought, or is it fiction ? Is it the Greatest Story Ever Told ? Or is it a load of plausible cobblers ? Is it true ? Or is it a monster hoax ? Almost impossible, he mumbled sadly, to tell these days.